Perfect Predators

Joanne Mattern

Rourke
Educational Media
rourkeeducationalmedia.com

www.rourkeeducationalmedia.com

PHOTO CREDITS: Cover: © jim kruger; Title Page: © Ammit; Page 2-3: © Iakov Filimonov; Page 4: © Greg Panosian, Creative Commons; ©; Page 5: © David Gomez; Page 6: © Ruta Bajorynaite-Balsiene; Page 7: © Andy Gehrig, Olaf Loose, Peter_Nile; Page 8: © Chris Kruger; Page 9: © Hans Peter (joan) Egert, Alfredo Maiquez; Page 10: © Maria Dryfhout, Archana Bhartia; Page 11: © Steven Love, Cathy Keifer, Creative Commons; Page 12: © Iryna Volina, Ricardo Reitmeyer, Graeme Purdy, 4FR, Hanquan Chen; Page 13: © fotografie4you.eu, Jeryl Tan, Andy Gehrig, chee Seng choi, brytta; Page 14: © Anke Van Wyk, Smellme; Page 15: © Jason Prince; Page 16: © Hudakore, Erik Bettini; Page 17: © Craig Dingle, Island Effects, Aleksandar Jaksic; Page 18: © Keith Flood; Page 19: © Deborah Coles, Planctonvideo, United States public domain; Page 20: © Ron Chapple, Greg Nicholas; Page 21: © Tamara Bauer; Page 22: © Creative Commons; Page 23: © Tammy Fullum;

Edited by Precious McKenzie

Cover Design by Renee Brady
Interior Design by Cory Davis

Library of Congress PCN Data

Perfect Predators / Joanne Mattern
(Eye to Eye with Animals)
ISBN 978-1-61810-118-1 (hard cover) (alk. paper)
ISBN 978-1-61810-251-5 (soft cover)
Library of Congress Control Number: 2011944409

Rourke Educational Media
Printed in the United States of America,
North Mankato, Minnesota

Also Available as:

Rourke
Educational Media
rourkeeducationalmedia.com
customerservice@rourkeeducationalmedia.com • PO Box 643328 Vero Beach, Florida 32964

Table of Contents

Chapter 1
Born to Kill

A **predator** is an animal that hunts and eats other animals. Predators are born to kill! Some predators are big and strong. Others are small. All of them have powerful tools that help them be perfect predators.

Lion

Piranha

BIG AND BAD

The polar bear is the largest predator on land. A polar bear weighs up to 1,540 pounds (700 kilograms).

Predators have special body parts that help them hunt and kill their **prey**. Many large predators have powerful jaws filled with sharp teeth. A wolf or jaguar's teeth can slice through **flesh** quickly.

Few Teeth, Many Teeth

A wolf has 42 teeth to last its whole life. If a wolf loses a tooth, another one will not grow back. Reptiles and sharks, however, can grow new teeth. A crocodile can go through 3,000 teeth during its lifetime.

Saltwater crocodile

Great white shark

Martial eagle

Birds of prey use their feet as weapons. Their feet have powerful claws called **talons**. The bird flies down to grab, crush, and carry its prey with its talons. Birds of prey also have sharp beaks. These beaks rip into flesh or **spear** fish right out of the water.

8

Predators play an important role in the food chain. They keep small animal and insect populations under control. Predators usually capture the slowest or weakest animals from a group. So, they weed out the weak animals of a species. This means that only the strongest of a species survives.

Eastern chanting goshawk

WATCH THOSE TALONS!

The Harpy eagle has the largest talons of any bird. These talons can be up to 2-1/2 inches (6-1/2 centimeters) long and are strong enough to kill adult monkeys.

Some animals use poison as a weapon. Poisonous snakes inject **venom** into their prey using sharp front teeth called **fangs**. Jellyfish use their poison **tentacles**, wasps use their poison stingers, and spiders have a venomous bite. They all kill their prey using their poison.

Diamondback rattlesnake

Jellyfish

Yellow Arizona wasp

Jumping spider eating fruit fly

INSECTS WITH A TWIST

Many insects bite, but only bees, ants, and wasps sting. A spider-hunting wasp can sting and kill a spider many times its size.

11

Chapter 2

Meet the Big Cats

Cats are some of the strongest predators in the world. There are 36 species of wild cats. All of them are **carnivores.** A cat's body is built to kill. Its jaws are short and powerful. It has sharp teeth that can grab and tear prey.

LENGTH: 5-8 feet (1.5-2.4 m)

WEIGHT: 330-500 lbs (150-227 kg)

LIFE SPAN: 10-14 years

RANGE: Africa

LION

LENGTH: 6 feet (1.8 m)

WEIGHT: 110-140 lbs (50-64 kg)

LIFE SPAN: 10-12 years

RANGE: Africa

CHEETAH

LENGTH: 4-9 feet (1.4-2.8 m)

WEIGHT: 400-675 lbs (181-306 kg)

LIFE SPAN: 10-15 years

RANGE: Southeast Asia, China, far eastern Russia

TIGER

MOUNTAIN LION

LENGTH: 3.5-5.5 feet (1-1.7 m)

WEIGHT: 110-180 lbs (50-82 kg)

LIFE SPAN: 12-25 years

RANGE: North and South America

JAGUAR

LENGTH: 5-8 feet (1.7-2.4 m)

WEIGHT: 100-250 lbs (45-113 kg)

LIFE SPAN: 15-20 years

RANGE: Central and South America

LEOPARD

LENGTH: 3-6 feet (.91-1.8 m)

WEIGHT: 82-200 lbs (37-91 kg)

LIFE SPAN: Up to 20 years

RANGE: Africa, Asia

SNOW LEOPARD

LENGTH: 6-7.5 feet (1.8-2.3 m)

WEIGHT: 77-120 lbs (35-55 kg)

LIFE SPAN: Up to 21 years

RANGE: Mountains of Central Asia

retractable claws

White Tiger

Cats also have amazing claws. Most cats have retractable claws. They can pull their claws in and out. Cats **retract** their claws while running. Then they leap onto their prey and **extend** their claws to kill.

SOLITARY HUNTERS

Most cats hunt alone. Lions are different. They live and hunt in large groups, called prides.

15

Chapter 3
Raging Reptiles

Reptiles are some of the most dangerous predators on Earth. Watch out because even small reptiles can be deadly. The Gila monster is a lizard that only weighs about 3 pounds (1.4 kilograms). But its poisonous bite can kill small animals.

Gila Monster

Gila Monster

The Komodo dragon is the largest and deadliest lizard of all. These lizards can grow up to 10 feet (3 meters) long! Komodo dragons live in Indonesia. They use their powerful jaws to kill large prey such as deer.

BIGGER AND BADDER

A Komodo dragon is the world's largest lizard, but it isn't the largest reptile. That honor goes to the saltwater crocodile. These crocs can be up to 17 feet (5 meters) long and weigh more than 3,000 pounds (1,361 kilograms).

Chapter 4
Predators at Sea

Many predators live in the ocean. Sharks are some of the fiercest sea creatures. A great white shark kills and eats large animals such as seals, dolphins, and sea lions. Sharks even attack people!

Great white shark

Squids and octopuses have great eyesight. They spot fish in the water and grab them with their long tentacles.

Squid

Octopus tentacles

FISHING FOR PREY

Female anglerfish have a long, skinny fin that sticks out of their mouth. This fin looks like a worm. When other fish come near to eat the "worm," the anglerfish surprises them and then grabs them and sucks them into her mouth.

19

Chapter 5

Predators in Danger!

Predators are fierce, but many of them are also **endangered**. Many predators have lost their **habitats** because people build houses, factories, and roads where the animals used to live. **Poachers** kill many predators for their fur or other body parts.

Turning the Tables

Predators can also be endangered because of other predators. An Australian predator called the quoll is in danger because people have introduced house cats and poisonous toads to their habitat. These new predators think the quoll is prey and have killed large numbers of them.

Endangered white tigers live in captivity at the Zoological Park in Singapore.

People are working hard to protect predators. Even though predators are born to kill, it's important to protect them from extinction. These fierce animals are an important part of the food chain and they keep nature in balance. They are amazing animals who are a vital part of our world.

Glossary

carnivores (KAR-nuh-vorez): animals that only eat meat

endangered (en-DANE-jerd): in danger of dying out

extend (ex-TEND): to stretch out

fangs (FANGZ): long, hollow teeth that inject venom

flesh (FLESH): the soft parts of the body that cover the bones, including fat and muscles

habitats (HAB-uh-tatz): places where an animal lives in the wild

poachers (POH-churz): people who hunt protected animals

predator (PREH-duh-tuhr): an animal that hunts and eats other animals

prey (PRAY): an animal that is eaten by another animal

retract (ree-TRAKT): to pull in

spear (SPEER): to grab something with a sharp object

talons (TAL-uhnz): long, sharp, curved claws found on birds of prey

tentacles (TEN-tuh-kuhlz): long, moving limbs that are used to feel and grab prey

venom (VEN-uhm): a poison produced by an animal

Index

Websites To Visit

animals.nationalgeographic.com/animals/big-cats/facts/

www.peregrinefund.org/subsites/explore-raptors-2001/

www.predatorconservationtrust.com/kids.htm

About the Author

Joanne Mattern has written hundreds of nonfiction books for children. She really loves learning about wild animals, so writing PERFECT PREDATORS was a great experience for her! Joanne grew up on the banks of the Hudson River in New York state and still lives in the area with her husband, four children, and an assortment of predator pets including a dog, cats, reptiles, and fish.

Meet The Author!
www.meetREMauthors.com